WEEKS PUBLIC LIBRARY
GREENLAND, N. H.
W9-CMZ-084

TO CELEBRATE
THE BIRTH OF
JACOB EDWARD
GALLANT
June 24, 1994
HAPPY BIRTHDAY!!
© 1987 GAYLORD

ANNA GROSSNICKLE HINES

Moompa, Toby, and Bomp

CLARION BOOKS · NEW YORK

Clarion Books
a Houghton Mifflin Company imprint
215 Park Avenue South, New York, NY 10003

Printed in the USA

Library of Congress Cataloging-in-Publication Data

Hines, Anna Grossnickle.
Moompa, Toby, and Bomp / written and illustrated by Anna Grossnickle Hines.
p. cm.
Summary: Moompa takes his young grandchild, Toby, and Toby's doll, Bomp, to the park, but when it's time to go home, Bomp is missing.
ISBN 0-395-61301-9
[1. Grandfathers—Fiction. 2. Parks—Fiction. 3. Lost and found possessions—Fiction. 4. Dolls—Fiction] I. Title.
PZ7.H572Mk 1993
[E]—dc20

92-5667
CIP
AC

WOZ 10 9 8 7 6 5 4 3 2 1

For Ivan
and all who love him

"Walk, Moompa," said Toby.

So they walked, Moompa,

Toby, and Bomp.

They walked to the park where
Moompa pushed Toby in the swing,

and Toby pushed Bomp.

Toby climbed up.

Bomp slid down.

Toby bounced in the grass.

Moompa watched.

Bomp flipped up.
“Up Bomp,” said Toby.

Toby bumped down.

"Uh oh," said Moompa.
"Uh oh," said Toby.

Toby dug in the sand.

Moompa said, "Toby! My feet are all gone."

"Ah gone." Toby laughed.

SF
49ERS

“Doots!” cried Toby. “Doots! Doots!”

"Ducks," said Moompa. "We have popcorn for the ducks."

"Popacup," said Toby. "Doots' popacup."
"Quack, quack," said the ducks.
"Kakyak," said Toby.

"It's time to go, Toby," Moompa said.
"Go," said Toby. "Bye bye, doots."
"Bye bye, ducks," said Moompa.

"Uh oh," said Toby. "Bomp ah gone."
"Where'd he go?" asked Moompa.
"Bomp go?" asked Toby.

Toby looked down.

Moompa looked up.

Toby looked in.

Moompa looked on.

Toby looked all around.

“Bomp!” squealed Toby.
“Bomp,” Moompa agreed.
“Safe and sound.”

"Let's go home," said Moompa.
"Go home," said Toby.
And so they did . . .

Moompa, Toby, and Bomp.
SF
49ERS